KEVIN CORNELL

GO TO SLEEP, MONSTER!

BALZER + BRAY

An imprint of Harper Collin

Balzer + Bray is an imprint of HarperCollins Publishers

Go to Sleep, Monster!
COPYRIGHT © 2016 BY KEVIN CORNELL
ALL RIGHTS RESERVED. MANUFACTURED IN CHINA.

FOR INFORMATION ADDRESS
HarperCollins Children's Books,
a division of HarperCollins Publishers
195 Broadway, New York, NY 10007
www.harpercollinschildrens.com

ISBN 978-0-06-234915-6

HAND LETTERING BY KEVIN CORNELL
16 17 18 19 SCP 10 9 8 7 6 5 4 3 2 1

For Mac and Steve...
...and Kim, who holds my hand.

"It's time to go to sleep!"

"I can't!" said George, "I'm afraid!

There's a monster under the bed!"

"Monster," said Anna, "stop scaring my brother!

It's time to go to sleep!"

"Sleep?" he said. "I can't sleep!

There's a monster under the floor!"

"Hey, monster," said Anna.
"Stop all this scaring!

It's time to go to sleep!"

"I wish I could sleep, but I can't!"
he replied.

"There's a monster under this room!"

"There's no monster down here,"
said George.

"Shhhhh! Be quiet!
There's a monster under the table!"

"Pssssst! Watch out!
There's a monster under the house!"

"...under the gravel!"

"...under the dirt!"

"In the center-most center...

...of the center of the earth!"

"Monster in the Center of the Earth," said Anna. "Stop scaring everyone!

It's time to go to sleep!"

"Sleep? Oh, no, I can't sleep!"
he said. "I'm much too afraid!"

"But you're the underest under
something someone can be!"
said Anna. "What's left for you
to be afraid of?!"

"I'm afraid of being alone!"

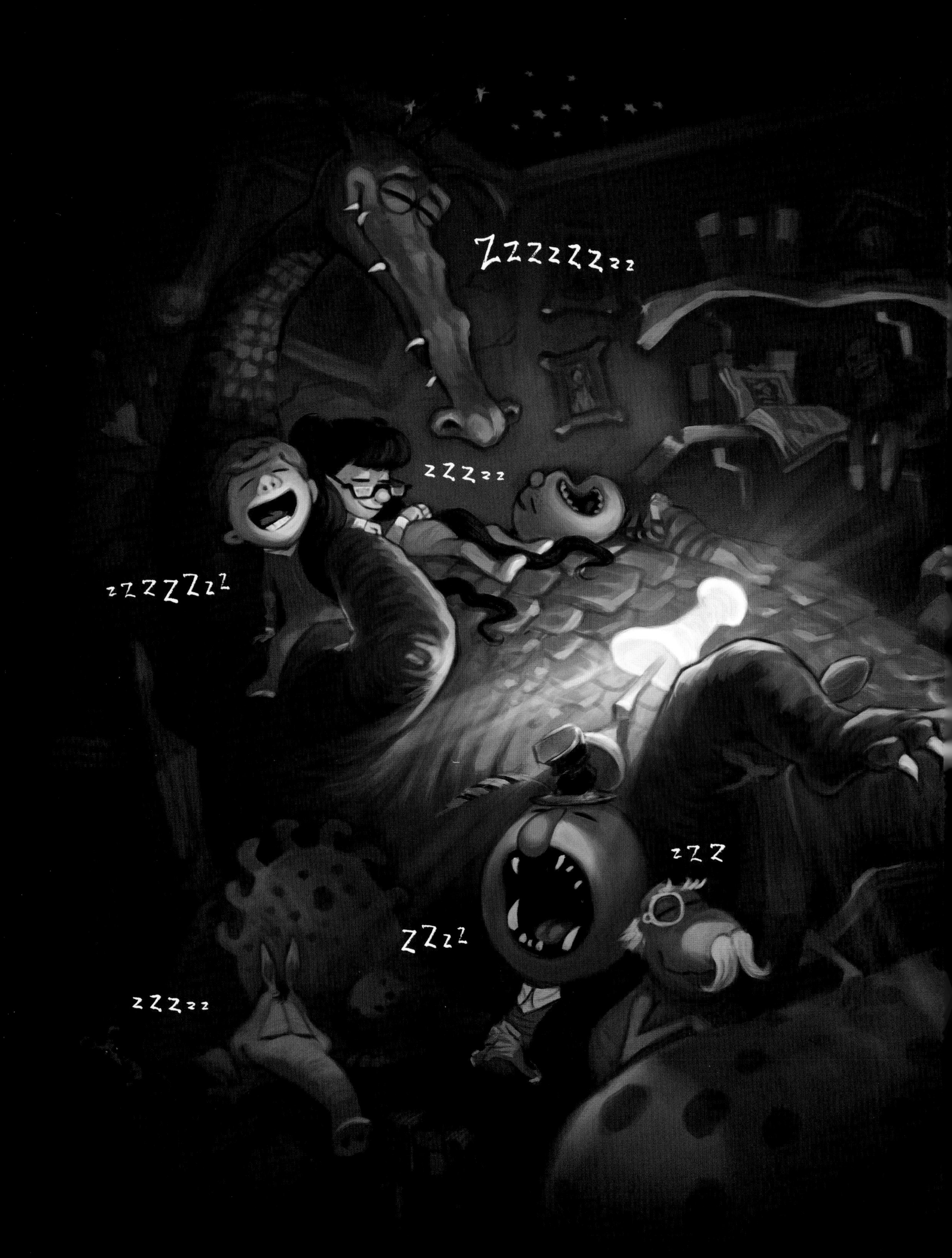

Zzzzzzzzz
zzzzz
zzzzzzzz
zzz
zzzz
zzzzz

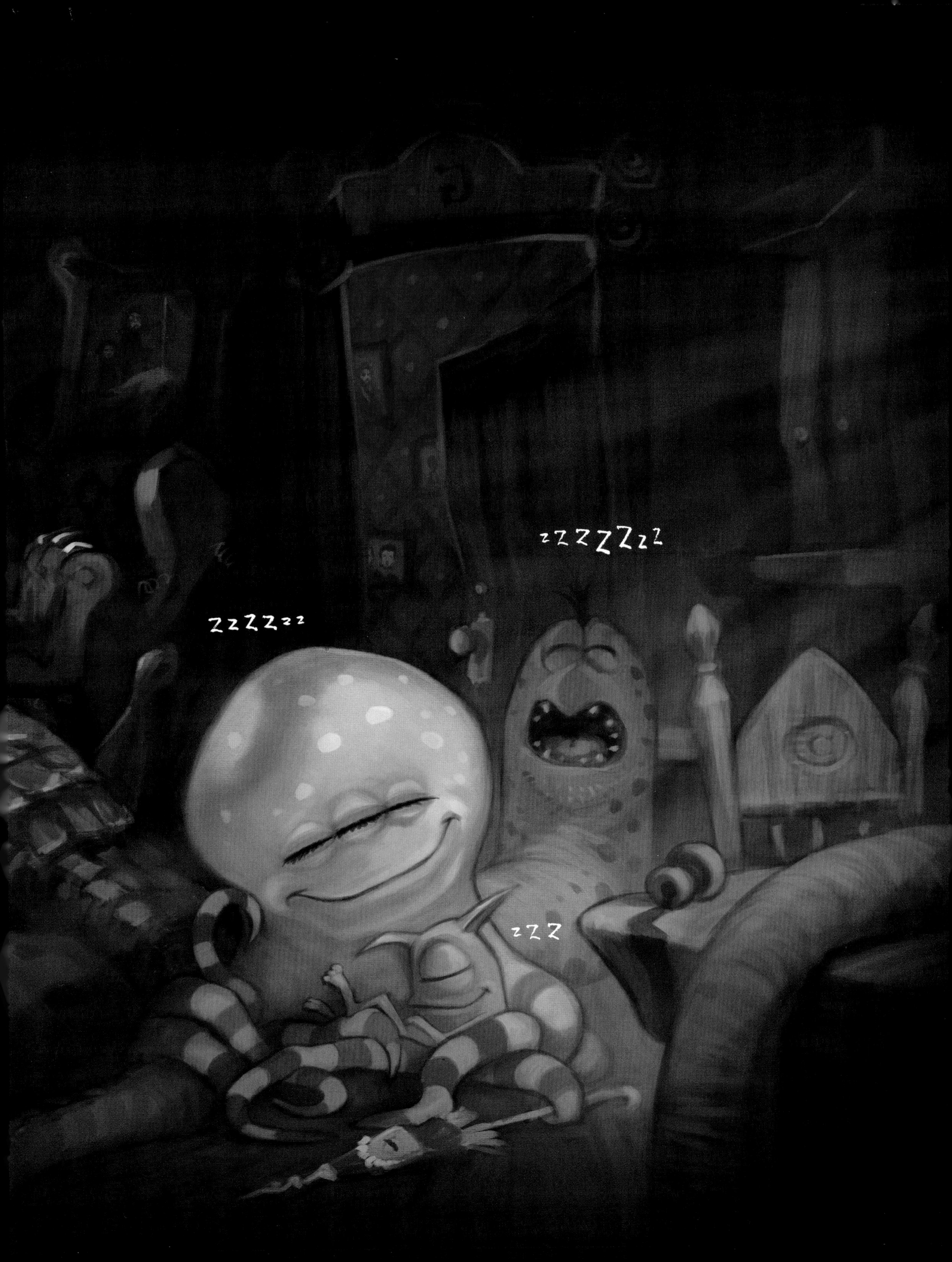
zzzZZzzz
zzZZzz
zzZ